293
Fea

cop. 1

FEAGLES
Thor and the giants

DATE DUE			
FEB 12 '75			
JAN 6 29			

SEATTLE PUBLIC SCHOOLS
Seattle, Washington

THOR AND THE GIANTS

Thor and the Giants

AN OLD NORSE LEGEND RETOLD
BY ANITA FEAGLES

WITH ILLUSTRATIONS BY
GERTRUDE BARRER-RUSSELL

NEW YORK
YOUNG SCOTT BOOKS

Long ago, when men believed in many gods, there was a
powerful god by the name of Thor. He had the strength
of many men, and his magic hammer could split mountains. Thor liked to travel, for there was nothing the gods
enjoyed more than adventure. One day he decided to take
a journey to a place called Utgard, for this was said to be
the home of the giants. Thor had always wanted to see
the land of the giants, and especially to meet their king, in
order to learn whether his power was as great as Thor's.
As a companion on this journey, Thor took his friend
Loki, another god. And so they set out in Thor's chariot,
which was drawn by two fine goats.

MAY -- 1969

The first night, they stopped at a peasant's hut and asked for food and shelter. The peasant said, "I have no food to give you, for I have not enough even to give supper to my wife and son tonight. But you are welcome to rest under my roof."

"We don't want to go without dinner," Loki said. "I am very hungry."

But Thor replied, "We can manage the food all right."

He and Loki went into the hut and met the peasant's wife and his son, Thialfe.

Thor said, "Thialfe, you may kill the goats that pull my chariot, and they shall be supper for all of us."

The peasant thought it a shame to kill two such fine beasts, but he was not one to argue with strangers, especially when they were going to give him and his family a fine meal, so the deed was done.

In the morning, just before they were ready to depart, Thor swung his magic hammer over the pile of goat bones, and to the peasant's amazement, there were the two goats again, as lively as ever.

Then Thor said, "I shall not need my chariot for the next part of the trip, so I'll leave it here with you. But in order to make certain that I find it the same as I left it when I return, Thialfe shall come with Loki and me on our journey. He seems to be a strong boy and may be useful to us."

Again, the peasant agreed, and Thialfe went along with
the two gods.

The three of them traveled until they came to a great sea.
"How are we going to get across this?" Loki asked.
Thor said, "We shall have to swim." And so without
another word, they all plunged into the water.

The peasant boy, being used to a hardy life, had scarcely any more trouble swimming across than the gods, and so they all reached the other shore without any difficulty.

There was nothing to be seen except big, jagged rocks and a forest off in the distance. By the time they reached the forest, it was pitch dark, and they couldn't see where they were going. They all held onto each other to avoid getting lost.

However, by luck they at last came upon some kind of shelter, and they went inside. They had had such a hard day's travel that after eating some grain from a pouch Thor had with him, they all fell asleep at once.

Before long, their sleep was interrupted by some strange thunderous noises outside, but since they did not know what the noises were or what to do about them, they decided to rest as best they could.

Still, they were glad to hear the cock crow in the morning. There seemed to be no windows in the shelter, but Thor found a wide opening in the wall through which they had entered last night. It was so big that he knew no door could have been found to fit it.

Once outside, the first thing Thor saw was an enormous giant asleep in the grass, and he knew at once that the sounds which had disturbed him and his companions last night were nothing more than the snores of the giant. Drawing his sword, Thor came up close to the giant. Just then, the giant opened his eyes and stared at Thor.

After a moment, Thor found his voice and said, "What is your name?"

The giant raised himself up on one elbow, which caused his head to go up so far that Thor thought it was taking flight altogether. The giant said, "My name is Skrymmer. And I believe you are the god Thor?"

"I am," Thor replied.

"Did you happen to pick up my glove?" the giant asked.

Thor realized that the shelter he and his friends had found was the giant's glove. He and the giant continued in friendly conversation, and when it turned out that they were all going to Utgard, the giant offered to accompany them.

"I am going to Utgard because it is my home," the giant said. "But why do you wish to make a visit there?"

"I am eager to meet the king," Thor replied. "I have heard that his power is great, and I have long wondered if it is as great as mine."

The giant made no reply to this, but he offered to carry their grain pouch in his knapsack. They continued on through the forest, the giant being careful to walk very slowly so they could keep up with him. They were still not out of the forest at nightfall, so they all settled down under a great oak tree. Skrymmer fell asleep at once and began snoring again. The rest of the group, however, were very hungry, and so they set to work to open Skrymmer's knapsack. But they could not even begin to untie the knot.

Loki said, "Thor, we cannot go without dinner. Something must be done."

Thor decided to awaken the giant, but he was not able to do this by any ordinary means, and so at last he picked up his magic hammer and threw it at the giant. But the giant only opened one eye and said, "Why are the leaves dropping off the trees?" And he began snoring again.

Thor picked up his hammer and this time hit him in the back of the head. The giant opened the other eye and said sleepily, "My, this dust is a nuisance!" And he began to snore again.

Thor was astonished, but still he decided to make one more try. He took up his hammer and struck the giant directly on the cheek. Skrymmer opened both eyes and brushed his cheek, saying, "There are birds around here, because I just felt a feather drop on me." And with that, he started snoring again.

By now, Thor was angry. "We have no choice but to go to sleep hungry," he said.

"Yes," Loki answered. "But I wonder why that monster is not also hungry. I myself am famished!"

In the morning, the giant said, "I am afraid I shall have to go on ahead of you now. I have already delayed my journey by walking so slowly, and I cannot delay longer."

"We have no wish to detain you," Thor said.

"It was kind of you to carry the grain pouch," Loki added. "But now we must have it back."

The giant returned the pouch with these words, "Before I go, let me give you some useful advice. You should give up your idea of going to Utgard. The people there are all as big as I am. You think too much of yourself, and you will take too much on yourself. If you are wise, you will stay away." And with that, the giant walked ahead of them and quickly disappeared into the forest.

"Why did he not tell us that before?" Thialfe asked.

"It would not have mattered," Thor said. "I am the mighty god Thor, and no one shall stop me from going where I wish!"

Soon they came within sight of the city walls, and as they got closer, the size of the gates and the city filled them with amazement. When they had actually walked under the gates, their wonder was beyond words, for the houses were so tall they had trouble seeing the top windows. The streets were so wide it was a long journey across them. A mouse ran across the street and Thialfe jumped, thinking it was a bear. But the mouse was more frightened than Thialfe, for it was being chased by a cat that was huge beyond belief. The people were as large as Skrymmer had said, and the three travelers had to take care not to get stepped on, for they were not even noticed.

Still, Thor had not forgotten who he was or what he intended to do, so they set out for the palace.

When they arrived, they asked to see the king. After a while they were ushered into his presence. But the king, whose name was Utgarda Loke, was expecting someone of a different size, and he did not even see Thor bowing and greeting him. When he at last glanced down and saw the group, he burst out laughing. The courtiers all joined in the laughter, too. When finally they stopped, Thor was able to make himself heard.

"We are small in comparison with you," he shouted. "But I am the god Thor, and these are my friends, Loki and Thialfe. We are gifted with powers that may surprise you."

"Really!" said Utgarda Loke, raising his eyebrows, and then he and his courtiers went into a laughing fit that lasted even longer than before.

Finally the king stopped, saying, "Well, we're willing to give these people a fair trial." And, pointing to Loki, he said, "Let's hear what you can do."

"Your Majesty, I am very good at eating," said Loki.

"It looks as if you'll have to grow a little before you can be very good at much of anything." And again the king and his courtiers burst out laughing, but meanwhile, the king's servants brought in a trough of food. Loki was placed at one end and one of the courtiers at the other. They both began eating, and met in the middle. But while Loki had eaten the meat, the courtier had also consumed the bones and the trough, so Loki was the loser.

The king turned to Thialfe next. "And what can you do?" he asked.

"I am thought to be a fast skater," Thialfe said.

"Try him," said the king. And so they all went to a field of smooth ice, and another skater was set against Thialfe. Thor and Loki saw that Thialfe was indeed a marvelous skater, swifter than any they had ever seen, and yet the giant glided past him so rapidly that he was back to the starting line before Thialfe had traveled even half the distance.

Then the king turned to Thor and said, "And now may I ask what you can do yourself?"

"I can drain a wine cup no matter how large it is," replied the god.

"Try him," said Utgarda Loke. And so the royal cup-bearer presented Thor with a drinking horn. "If you are any good, you will finish it in one swallow," said the king. "Some people have to take two swallows, but the weakest person here can do it in three."

Thor took up the horn, and being very thirsty, took a long swallow. He thought he had done very well, but on removing it from his lips he was astounded to see how much was left.

A second time he drank, but the wine hardly went down. After the third swallow, the horn still seemed almost full to the brim. So he put it down in despair, admitting that he could not drink it all.

"I am disappointed in you," Utgarda Loke said. "I can see there's no use asking you to play men's games, so I must try you at a child's game."

"Now you shall try to lift my cat from the ground,"
said the king.

Just then a big cat came leaping along and stood before
Thor, looking none too friendly. Still, Thor grabbed it, but
in spite of his efforts he was only able to lift one paw from
the ground.

"Pooh! Pooh!" exclaimed the king. "I see you are not even a child, but a mere infant. My old nurse would be more than a match for you. Come nursey, and wrestle with the mighty god Thor!"

An old lady came forth then, with white hair and many wrinkles. She came toward Thor and tried to throw him to the ground, but though he used all the strength he had, he was surprised to find that he could hardly keep his footing. For some time, he withstood her, but at last she brought him to one knee, and this time he had to admit that he was defeated.

Ashamed, the three travelers left the palace and went to find a place to stay for the night. In the morning, just as they were getting ready to leave the city, the king sent for them. He entertained them with a fine feast. After they had eaten their fill, he said to Thor, "Now tell me honestly. What do you think of your success here?"

"I am astounded and ashamed," Thor said.

"I knew you were," the king said. "But now that it's all over, I'll tell you a couple of secrets. You've been fooled by magic ever since you came here. I am the giant you met on the way. I tried to discourage you from coming here when I saw that you had more power than I thought. The three blows you gave me with your magic hammer would have killed me if they had really hit me. But it was a huge mountain you struck at, not I, and if you return there, you will see that you made three valleys in the mountains with your hammer.

"The courtier who consumed the food against Loki was no ordinary giant, but Fire, which can destroy everything. Thialfe's enemy was not a skater, but Thought, and no matter how fast anyone may move, he cannot outrun Thought. As for yourself, the drinking horn was the sea, and we were surprised that you drank as much as you did. The gray cat was as heavy as the earth itself, and we were amazed that you could lift one paw.

"But your last feat was the most wonderful of all, for the old nurse was none other than Death, and I have never seen anyone over whom Death had so little power."

"And so, my friends, you may go now, but I must ask you never to come back, and if you try I shall do my best to prevent you from reaching here."

Then the king vanished.

"Wait!" cried out Thor, but now the city had vanished also. The four travelers found themselves in a pleasant meadow with a stream running through it. And so they started back toward home with much to say about their remarkable adventure.

About The Author

ANITA MACRAE FEAGLES graduated from Knox College in Galesburg, Illinois, and took her M.S. at City College in New York. Her extensive travels have taken her to more than forty-five countries. Among them was Iceland, where her interest in Viking legends developed.

She has written many books for children. Most recently, William R. Scott, Inc. has published her re-telling of the famous epic of Gilgamesh, *He Who Saw Everything,* and a thirteenth century Viking legend called *Autun And The Bear.*

Mrs. Feagles lives in Chappaqua, New York, with her husband and four children.

About The Artist

GERTRUDE BARRER-RUSSELL's paintings and ceramic work have been exhibited in museums and galleries in many parts of the country. Her versatility and style as an artist are revealed in her two previous books for children, *For Alice A Palace* and *Autun And The Bear,* both published by William R. Scott, Inc.

She and her husband, artist-photographer Frank Russell, live in Roxbury, Conn. They have two daughters and numerous cats.